Chaos at the Café

AA Published by AA Publishing.

This book belongs to

_____

© Automobile Association
Developments Limited 2005

AA Publishing is a trading name of
Automobile Association Developments Limited,
Fanum House, Basing View, Basingstoke, Hampshire RG21 4EA.
Registered number 1878835

A CIP catalogue record for this book is available from The British Library

ISBN 0-7495-4701-4
978-0-7495-4701-1
A02616

Printed and bound in China.

Chaos at the Café

Written by Victoria Kingsbury

One day, Patrolman Pete was enjoying a sunny afternoon sitting outside the roadside café waiting for his favourite snack – a cheese and chutney sandwich.

"Oh, what a lovely day," he said to Trevor the Toolbox. "Have we any call outs to go to?"

"No, it's been a quiet day so far," replied Trevor.

Just then, they heard a strange noise coming from the café – Christos was singing!

Christos was busy cooking. He loved to sing while he cooked and today he was singing very loudly.

"It's a lovely day, isn't it Christos?" shouted Pete.

There was no answer. Christos was singing so loudly that he couldn't hear a thing.

"He's in a world of his own, isn't he?" Pete said to Trevor.

In fact, Christos was in such a dream that he hadn't noticed that the toffee he had been making for toffee apples was now starting to bubble over the pot.

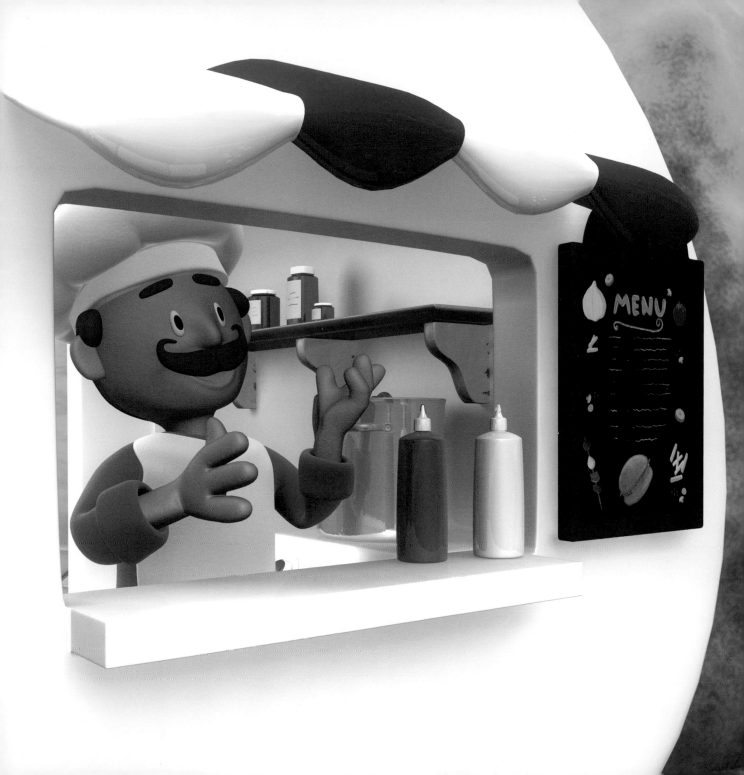

The toffee had bubbled over so much that it was now running over the cooker, onto the floor, through the back door and onto the road outside. The toffee was very sticky and the cars on the road were starting to get stuck. The drivers looked very cross!

"What's going on?" one of them shouted.

"My wheels won't go round!" said another.

"It looks like it's coming from the café. I'll call for help on my mobile 'phone," said the first driver.

All this time Pete had been sitting on the other side of the café and he couldn't see the sticky toffee on the road. Just then, there was a voice on the radio.

"Pete, are you there?" asked the voice.

It was Rita at the call centre. She had just had a call from a very cross driver about the toffee on the road.

"Hello Rita, how can I help?" asked Pete.

"The road outside the café is covered in toffee and the cars are getting stuck in it. Can you go and help them out?" asked Rita.

"Righto Rita! We're already there. Thanks for the call," said Pete.

Pete ran round to the road, which was now covered with toffee. The toffee was so sticky that it had stuck the cars to the road like extra strong glue! Stan came over to Pete to see what he could do to help.

"This is very dangerous!" said Pete. "Stan, you go to the back of the traffic queue to slow the cars down and warn them of the danger ahead."

"Pete, we need to tell Christos what's going on. I can still hear him singing in there," Trevor shouted.

Pete ran over to the café to tell Christos that his pan of toffee was bubbling over.

"Christos! Christos! Are you alright?" shouted Pete.

Christos was walking back towards the café. He had just taken the rubbish out and when he turned round he saw Pete running towards him.

"What's happening?" gasped Christos.

Suddenly, Christos remembered that he'd left his toffee on the cooker.

"Oh no, the toffee!" he shouted, "I forgot all about it."

Christos ran into the café and carefully took the pan of toffee off the cooker and carried it outside.

"Well done, Christos," said Pete. "Now I had better go and see what's happening on the road."

"Oh no!" cried Christos. "I hope it hasn't caused too much trouble."

Pete ran back to the road to find Trevor and Stan. They had been working hard, washing all the toffee away.

"Well done," said Pete. "Now all we need to do is to change the tyres on the cars so that they can move again."

"Ready for action, Pete!" said Trevor. "Stan has got the spare tyres ready."

Pete took off the tyres that were sticky with toffee and put on the new ones in no time. Soon everyone was happy again.

"You're ready to roll!" said Stan to the drivers. "The road is now clear, so move along slowly please."

The drivers were very grateful and they waved to Pete, Trevor and Stan as they drove off.

Once everyone had got over the commotion, Pete wondered how Christos was feeling.

"I'd better go and see if Christos is alright," said Pete. "He must be a bit upset."

"I'll come too," said Trevor.

"I'll stay here for a while and make sure the road clears," said Stan.

Back at the café, Pete found Christos looking very upset.

"I've caused so much trouble," he said.

"Don't worry," said Pete, "we all make mistakes. Just try to concentrate on one thing at a time in future."

Just then, they heard a "beep beep." It was Stan coming towards them.

"Well done everybody! The road is clear and all the traffic is running smoothly," said Stan.

Pete's tummy started to rumble.

"I'd forgotten all about my cheese and chutney sandwich," he said. "I'm hungry!"

Christos started to say, "I don't suppose you'd like a sticky toffee apple to say thank..."

"NO THANKS," they all chuckled, shaking their heads.

"I think we've all had enough sticky toffee for one day, don't you?" said Pete.

A Tall Tale

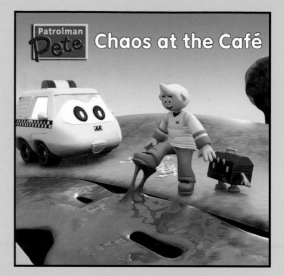

Chaos at the Café

Collect all of the Patrolman Pete adventures!

Stan Gets Wet

A Windy Day